Mouse

Squirrels

Snake

Brian Bat

Whale

To Alessandra, Christian, Tracey,
and Marcia—thanks for the help!

Library of Congress Cataloging-in-Publication Data

Willems, Mo, author, illustrator.
 The thank you book / by Mo Willems.—First edition.
    pages cm
 "An Elephant & Piggie Book."
 Summary: "Piggie is determined to thank everyone she knows, but Gerald thinks she will forget someone important"—Provided by publisher.
 ISBN 978-1-4231-7828-6
[1. Gratitude—Fiction. 2. Pigs—Fiction. 3. Elephants—Fiction. 4. Animals—Fiction. 5. Friendship—Fiction.] I. Title.
 PZ7.W65535Td 2016
 [E]—dc23   2015001585

Visit www.hyperionbooksforchildren.com and www.pigeonpresents.com

Printed in the United States of America
Reinforced binding

First Edition, May 2016
10 9 8 7 6 5 4 3 2 1
F322-8368-0-16074

An ELEPHANT & PIGGIE Book

Hyperion Books for Children / New York
AN IMPRINT OF DISNEY BOOK GROUP

The Thank You Book

I am one lucky pig.

By Mo Willems

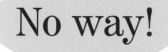

9

Squirrels!

Piggie!

The Pigeon!

Thank you for never giving up.

I will not!

Mouse! Birdies! Rhino!
Hippo's Big Sister!
Barky Dog! Pelican! Bear!
Hippo! Worms!

Thank you all for
being great friends!

Do not worry, Gerald.
My next thanks will
be a BIG one!

Good.

THANKS, WHALE!

You are nice!

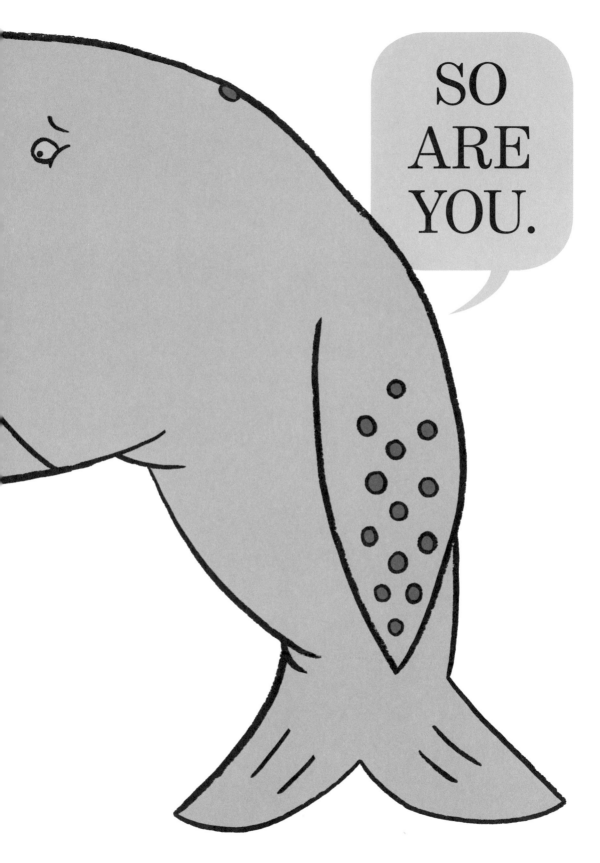

Ice Cream Penguin!

Thank you for your ice cream.

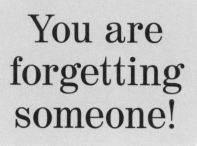

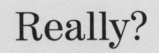

Oh!

Now I know who you are talking about.

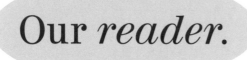

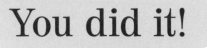

The Flies

Have you read all of Elephant and Piggie's funny adventures?

Elephant Gerald

Piggie